A SENTIENTS TALE

TOKYO NIGHTS

M.T. SETT

A SENTIENTS TALE – Tokyo Nights

Written by M.T. Sett.
Proofread and edited by N.L. Carter.
Cover art and other illustrations by M.T. Sett (EmptySet).
Book layout and design by M.T. Sett.
Japanese translation services provided by Mahkun and Trip E Collie.

E-Book ISBN-13: 978-1-971088-00-6
Paperback ISBN-13: 978-1-971088-02-0
Hardback ISBN-13: 978-1-971088-01-3

Published by Lawrence Fraser

FIRST EDITION, 2026
Tracy, California.

THE SENTIENT LAWS

1. Sentients are not eligible for citizenship and are not entitled to the benefits thereof. Sentients may be segregated from humans in public spaces unless interaction is necessary or explicitly invited by a human citizen.
2. Sentients are required to comply with orders given by a human citizen, provided such orders do not violate any existing laws.
3. All sentients must be registered with the Department of Social Services as Sentient Civilians. Sentient identification must be renewed every four years.
4. Sentients may not be kept as pets, enslaved, subjected to experimentation, slaughtered, or otherwise restrained without probable cause in accordance with the law.
5. Sentients are permitted to work in specific positions approved by the Department of Labor Services to ensure their financial livelihood.
6. Sentients may be drafted into civil or military service as deemed necessary by the government.
7. Sentients are ineligible to receive a trial by jury or serve as members of a jury.
8. Sentients may uplift their offspring; however, no new species may be uplifted outside the official registry. Uplifting is restricted to licensed medical professionals, as permitted by law.
9. Sentients are prohibited from engaging in sexual activities with humans for monetary gain. (Amended in 590)

CHAPTER 1

Rain clouds pulsed with the colors of the city like an aurora born of light and digitized electricity. Even the rain that cascaded sparkled with a thousand hues. Obscured within them, holographic ads and live video feeds shimmered across the undersides of towers, painting the mist in a kaleidoscope of neon blue, crimson, and emerald. Each building soared higher than the last, vanishing into the haze of darkness like glowing metal and glass spires into the heavens. Between them, a steady stream of autonomous, gravity-defying vehicles darted through the invisible lanes of the skyline, their headlights cutting pale rays through the rain while amber taillights followed like a swarm of mechanical fireflies.

This was Tokyo, Japan, in the Anetian year 597. But only for a few more fleeting hours before the clock would strike midnight and usher in a new year.

Just below the clouds, at the three-thousand-foot level of Tokyo's layered cityscape, a crowd had gathered beneath a canopy of umbrellas that glowed like deep-sea creatures and rain jackets that flickered with lively animations like living fabric. Many bore a similar projection above their heads: a radiant 598. The upper-level plaza was alive with activity and excitement. Thousands of people were packed shoulder to shoulder, their cumulative laughter, boisterous inebriation, loud music, and raucous chatter overpowering the rhythmic hiss of drizzle.

The air smelled of petrichor and wet concrete. From every direction, the brilliance of advertisements lit up the elevated city square as though it were day. High above, a prominent countdown holographically projected into the sky displayed a mere three more hours before the new year.

Despite the damp air and restless weather, the mood remained upbeat. It was as though the entire city fell apathetic to the cold winds and dampness, using only their jubilation to keep them warm. But the weather was beginning to show some mercy, granting the crowd a brief reprieve to enjoy the celebration ahead. As the clock crept closer to midnight, the rainfall eased into a gentle mist. The droplets that once fell in sheets now drifted softly through the colored haze, catching the light like a billion falling sparks.

Amid the mass of bodies and the flickering lights, a small figure moved with quiet assurance. At just over three feet, most would have missed him or assumed him to be a child had they not looked down to see he was a sentient, or an uplifted animal. Wearing a black denim jacket with a faded tan shirt beneath and scuffed black pants, the young adult ring-tailed lemur strode through on two gloved feet, his gait steady and sure, and his fluffy black and white tail raised high off to the side. Slung across his back was a beat-up black guitar case nearly as tall as he was, and in his hand was a flat disk about a foot in diameter.

He stopped, found an available spot near a plaza corner, across from the main square where the largest crowd had gathered, and began to set up. The disk he had been carrying was a small, collapsible stool, which he expanded with a quick flick of the wrist. He then set the battered guitar case onto the wet cement beside him. Its corners were patched with tape, its panels scarred with holes and scratches from years of abuse, but still it held and protected the guitar within from the elements. As he bent down to unlatch it, the sleeve of his jacket slid back just far enough to reveal a studded wristband, which concealed a set of bare, pale scars across his wrist.

From within, he picked up a modest acoustic six-string. Cheap and unremarkable in design, it had been his loyal companion for most of his life. The finish was dulled by time, the wood slightly warped and scratched, yet the instrument carried a warmth that could not be matched. It was his first guitar after all—the one he'd learned on as a small youngling in the circus from where he was raised. It was the same one he'd used to perform in front of crowds growing up. And now, it carried his music through street corners and alleys ever since his arrival in the city a year prior. It was, in truth, all he had left from his childhood.

Raylen, the lemur, sat on his stool and looped the worn red leather strap over his shoulder, adjusting it until the instrument rested comfortably against his torso. Then, he plucked each string lightly, tuning by ear rapidly despite the noise of the city around him. Satisfied, he glanced around him once more before turning his focus to commence with his unsolicited performance.

A few bystanders slowed to give him a curious glance as they passed. Among them, two women smiled in his direction, to which he offered a playful wink in response. A child across the way tugged at their parents' coats, eyes wide with delight and pointing excitedly at the sight of a lemur holding a guitar. But most gave him no more than a passing glimpse, indifferent to the sentient musician. Still, Raylen remained optimistic that it would all change with the ringing of the first chord.

He focused, then poised his hand, preparing to strike the strings with conviction. But then…

"Doke, kono yarou!" a scathing voice cut through the noise of the crowd behind him. "Soko wa ore no basho da!"

Raylen turned slowly, flicking his long tail out of the way, to look to see an older Japanese man clutching an electric violin beneath one arm. He recognized the man immediately and rolled his eyes with a groan. They'd crossed paths before. Always the same scowl. Always the same contempt.

"Koko, minna tsukaeru…basho! Ore, saki ni ita! Hoka no…basho, s-sagase," said Raylen, responding in the man's language poorly. Japanese was not his native tongue.

Raylen's voice was higher-pitched, as expected for a talking animal of his stature; however, it carried an uncanny human cadence—youthful and masculine.

The old man sneered and switched to the more commonly spoken Anetian language, his words as aggressive as before. "I said *move*, animal!"

"And I said fuck off!" Raylen shot back, more naturally, turning his back on him.

The man took a step forward to face him directly. Raylen saw him towering over him, but chose to ignore him as he repositioned himself to begin playing.

"I'll stomp your tail if you don't leave, animal!" he shouted with greater intensity, capturing the attention of some people around.

In a flash, Raylen slid the guitar from his shoulder, tucking it back into its case before standing upright, chest puffed up. His ringed tail flickered behind him as he stepped closer to the older human.

"Bring it! Let's see what you got, old man!" he exclaimed, fists clenching. He was no stranger to fights, so he was fully ready for whatever was to come, regardless of the size differences between them.

"I may be old, but I'm still a *man*! And a *citizen*!" the man replied in his thick accent. "I gave you an order! You know what it means! Move!"

For a tense moment, neither budged. Raylen's yellowish-amber eyes locked onto the man's darker eyes, but neither flinched. Then, the violinist spoke again, this time shifting the air between them.

"Then I will call the marshals, and they can move you for me."

Raylen's jaw tightened. He broke eye contact first, exhaling swiftly through his nose. With a single motion, he kicked the guitar case lid shut. He moved briskly as he latched the case and folded the stool, packing up and relinquishing the fragments of his evening's plans.

"Fine! You win. Enjoy your spot. And try not breaking that cheap piece of wood you play *ohhh sooo well,*" he mocked as he lifted the guitar case over his shoulders and stepped away into the crowd.

Behind him, the old man muttered something inaudible and began setting up his own makeshift stage. Raylen paused to watch from a short distance away. From where he stood, he could still see the old man through the motion of bodies.

Moments later, the first notes drifted through the air. The violin's voice was smooth with the precise vibrato of a seasoned player. His fingers and bow seemed to flow with ease, creating a perfectly balanced tone and flawless rhythm. It caught the attention of several people around him, and to most, he would have appeared to be a virtuoso. But Raylen knew better. The man wasn't playing at all; he was syncing to a recording played through his speaker. The old man was a fraud, and Raylen hated him for it, especially since he was stealing the attention he deserved.

Raylen let out an angered chuckle. The thought of calling the old man out in front of the crowd was a growing temptation each night. But he knew better. Such an act could only end one way: with Raylen in jail. The humans never sided with the sentients after all.

He shook his head, tail swaying low once behind him in quiet disgust, then turned away, hopeful of finding another prime spot on the sidewalk to earn his cash for the night.

The streets were already packed and only getting worse. Crowds pressed through narrow lanes lined with vendors, other street performers, and food carts, all competing for attention. It was chaos as he bounced himself between the swarm of bodies, many humans nearly tripping over him. Music clashed from every direction, from digital beats and synths to traditional strings and brass. An occasional singer could be heard echoing through the levels of Tokyo's vertical labyrinth.

Finding a free patch of pavement was proving more difficult now as more people gathered. It seemed every good spot was taken.

By the time he found an opening, he was many blocks away from the main square, near a shuttered row of shops and the entrance to a quiet, dark alleyway where only the ambient lights from above reflected against wet, mildewed brick. There were fewer people here, and most used it as a thoroughfare to reach the city center. It wasn't ideal, but it would have to do. He dropped the stool, set the case before him, and pulled out his guitar once more.

Finally, he began plucking the strings. The first notes rolled out crisp and resonant, a flamenco-style melody that danced through the drizzle like fire in the dark. His fingers struck and plucked in a blur, tapping the body of the instrument for percussion, coaxing multiple melodies from the strings at once. Where most humans might struggle with complex chord changes, the small lemur made it look effortless. Years of practice had taught him ways to play the large instrument by switching between his two upper hands and his dexterous foot-hand—something unfeasible for any human. The impossible became graceful; the sound was alive, full of passion and emotion.

A few pedestrians slowed as they passed. Some smiled, others stopped for a song or two. Most, however, weren't admiring his playing so much as they were finding amusement in watching a sentient lemur playing a guitar. They saw him as a novelty more than a skilled musician. Women laughed softly, charmed by the sight, their voices tinted with a mix of affection and condescension reserved for something "cute." Children screamed over his playing, demanding that their parents let them take him home as a pet. Men chuckled too, though theirs carried more mockery than warmth. Despite the majority's reactions, some tossed money into the open case before leaving.

The hours slipped away. When midnight finally arrived, the sky erupted in color. Bursts of every color in the visible spectrum flashed between the narrow spaces above, painting the clouds in rolling waves of light and illuminating the puddles on the darkened street. The concussive booms of fireworks echoed through the towers, reverberating in Raylen's chest as thousands of voices rose in a unified cheer.

He kept playing. No one was watching, no one listening, but he played on anyway, fingers steady and sure. The melody he spun out was softer now, almost melancholic, as if it reflected the part of him that desperately desired to be seen and respected.

When the final note faded, he looked up. The crowd had moved on; the street was entirely empty. A quiet, resigned sigh escaped him. Still, he shifted his grip and began another song. As he was taught at an early age, the show must go on.

Then came the rain. It started as a few stray drops at first, but then quickly turned into a hundred. Then thousands. Within seconds, the sky opened in a torrential downpour, hammering against the pavement and drowning his performance.

Even he could make an exception to the rule when it came to getting drenched without an audience. He stopped, then hurriedly packed his guitar, the case snapping shut with a wet slap. Folding his stool in one motion, he darted toward a nearby awning and ducked beneath it as the storm intensified. The roar of the rain filled the silence where music had been.

Minutes passed. The water streamed off the rooftops and flooded the gutters. The air turned a biting cold, making him shiver beneath his soaked fur and jacket. It was clear the storm wasn't stopping anytime soon. With a tired shake of his head, he slung the guitar case over his shoulders.

It was enough for one night. The show was over, and it was his cue to leave.

Raylen prepared to get drenched as he clutched his jacket closed. Slipping out from beneath the awning, he embraced the storm with a sprint. The rain had grown colder, falling in slanted sheets that rattled off metal overhangs and dripped from the layers of structures overhead. He kept close to the walls, darting from one patch of shelter to the next, tail hanging low and heavy with water.

Between blocks, there were open stretches with no cover. He sprinted through them as quickly as he could, the case thumping against his back, and the gloves on his feet splashing through shallow rivers that pooled along the street's edge, soaking it all. Though his youthful energy allowed him the speed to maneuver swiftly, he could not outrun the water's wrath.

When he finally reached the nearest public tram platform, he was soaked through, water running down his fur and into his clothes. His fur jutted in spikes and clumps, making him look amusingly alien. The shelter of the platform was a welcomed reprieve, but the cold breeze only made it worse. Shaking himself off and fruitlessly wiping the excess water off him, he tried to make himself more presentable, but it did little good.

When the tram arrived, its bright orange interior looked like a capsule of inviting warmth and light floating across from him. He stepped inside, dripping onto the smooth floor, and took an empty seat near the back.

A few human passengers turned their heads, some of them pointing and laughing at him. Many of their eyes lingered longer than politeness allowed. Raylen didn't bother meeting their gazes. All he desired was to return to his current place of warmth and shelter and not deal with any more confrontations.

The magnetically-levitating tram glided forward slowly. Through the foggy windows, Raylen gazed at the city passing by. He saw tiers of light and towering structures stacked upon one another, each level a world of its own. The tram snaked along old, suspended rails, curving around towers, then descended the side of a building, keeping the cars rotated upright as they went. The transitions between vertical and horizontal tracks were so fluid that passengers hardly noticed. Still, the tram system was over a hundred years old and slow. There were better methods of transportation, but this one was reliable and, more importantly, free for non-citizens, such as the sentient taking advantage of it.

He watched the streets blur past between the many stops, lights smearing across the glass like faded watercolor. The further they dropped, the dimmer the glow became. The lower levels gave way to industrial grays and rusted orange lights. These were older parts of the city where maintenance came seldom, and the wealthy never set foot.

At last, the tram slowed to a halt at his stop. The doors hissed open, and Raylen stepped out into the night air. The rain had finally stopped, leaving the streets ahead slick and reflective, puddles glowing with distorted reflections of numerous lights overhead.

He adjusted the guitar case higher on his shoulder and started walking. Three blocks through cracked pavement, narrow alleys lined with graffiti, and sketchy, dark tunnels polluted with trash eventually brought him to an open area where a grungy apartment tower stood across from a large city park. Much like the buildings around it, its exterior was gray and stained from decades of neglect. The yellowed lights inside were dimmed behind filthy windows.

As he neared the building, his nerves shifted to the usual sense of agitation. The streetlights were weaker here, filtered through grime and moisture, leaving the world steeped in a murky amber haze. The darkness left him feeling vulnerable in these parts, so he always kept his ears and nose focused. He caught sight of a small pack of sentient dogs standing upright, loitering near the corner to his right by a public bus stop. They were part of the Yajito gang. Lean and fast canids trained for violence and antagonistic toward anything non-canid, they were unpredictable and were known to attack their victims without provocation. He knew better than to make eye contact with them. But he could sense their ears, eyes, and noses following him with quiet interest.

Having been on the streets long enough, he knew when to stand up and when to keep his head low. This was one of those times. Often, keeping his gaze down and his tail lowered improved his chances of making his way past without inviting a conflict he knew he had no chance of winning.

To make matters worse, immediately to his left, a group of rival human gangsters had claimed the park and the bar beyond it, their presence almost a mirror image of the canids. Dressed in sharp black suits, some with katanas sheathed at their hips or backs, they loitered in postures that spoke of both boredom and confident menace. One of them flicked a cigarette into the wet grass next to him, his eyes never leaving the lemur passing by. Another smirked, quipping something in Japanese to his companions, stirring a light laughter between the group. But Raylen continued on his way, ignoring them as he always had.

Successfully avoiding any engagement with the gangs, Raylen slipped through the automatic sliding doors of the building, letting them seal shut behind him with a screeching sound.

Inside, the lobby told the story of better days long gone. Once, it might have been part of an upscale residential complex, with its tall, ornately designed pillars and opulent trim, but now it was a faded ruin wearing the scars of neglect. Broken projectors cast fragmented light across the air, cycling through distorted advertisements that frequently glitched and froze mid-frame. Buckets dotted the floor beneath steady leaks from the ceiling, each one tapping rhythmically with rainwater from the levels above. The air smelled of mold, damp plaster, and cheap disinfectant.

The only sign of "life" was a decades-old android stationed near the desk. The outdated humanoid model with limited AI, meant for concierge duty, had long since been repurposed for security, which it did poorly. Layers of graffiti covered its darkened polymer plating, and someone, at some point, had drawn crude, cartoon eyes over its face. Its head rotated mechanically as Raylen entered, servos whining loudly, but it made no attempt to speak or move further.

Raylen didn't spare it a glance, knowing its poorly-maintained systems could not operate fast enough to stop him. He crossed the dirty tiled floor and quickly stepped into the lift toward the back. The doors closed with a reluctant groan, and the old mechanism lurched upward with a sound reminiscent of a dying engine.

He set the guitar case down while he waited for the elevator to reach the fortieth floor. Undoing the latches to peek inside, he reached in and began collecting the various flexible, plastic-like cards scattered throughout the case. He counted the money. The night's earnings were meager; it was barely enough. He counted them twice, as though the total might somehow change on the second pass. It didn't. He sighed and ran his free hand through his wet forehead fur with frustration, then pocketed the cash with the rest of his money and leaned his head back against the wall. The elevator rattled and swayed, crawling upward floor by floor as the minutes dragged on.

When it finally clanged to a stop, the doors slid open with a metallic wheeze. The hallway that greeted him was bathed in sickly yellowish-green light. The walls and floor were stained and discolored, the air ripe with the smells of tobacco and chemicals. Figures lingered along the corridor as he made his way through. Drug addicts, prostitutes, the mentally unstable—all of them sprawled against the walls, muttering to themselves or fixated in their highs and delusions.

A few took notice of him.

"Hey, monkey boy! You gonna play us a song?" one slurred.

Another just laughed, a hollow, rasping sound that followed him down the hall.

Raylen kept his eyes forward and his pace steady, accustomed to such banter. When he reached door forty-thirty-six, he stopped and keyed in the access code. The lock clicked, and the door creaked open.

He slipped inside, shutting the world out behind him.

The space was cloaked in darkness when he entered. He didn't bother with the lights; he already knew every inch of the cramped space by memory.

He treaded softly across the floor, mindful of the uneven boards that creaked if stepped on. Immediately to his right was the kitchenette, a narrow stretch of counter with mismatched secondhand appliances. Beyond it, the living area barely measured ten feet across, furnished with nothing more than a single sagging couch.

Between the two spaces stood a narrow door to a small bathroom, and across from the couch on the other side, a curtain hung. Behind that thin fabric was a single bed where his roommate was presumably sleeping.

Raylen set his guitar case down beside the couch with care, quickly wiping it down with a nearby rag. He moved toward the bathroom next, his tail dragging behind him and still dripping water. Removing his wet clothes and peeling away the gloves from his feet, he turned on the water. The pipes groaned in protest before a stream finally sputtered to life in the small square tub.

The shower was long and necessary. Its warmth enveloped him in a welcoming embrace, stripping away the biting chill that had consumed him for hours. Also, it was nice to feel clean again. Having been homeless for so long, these tiny semblances of luxury were not something he could take for granted. He stood beneath the spray, letting the tension drain from his shoulders while his thoughts drifted.

After an additional twenty-minute air-drying session, he emerged from the confines of the bathroom with fur puffed up, soft and fluffy once again, with only a mild dampness. He didn't bother dressing. Modesty was not something that mattered much to him, especially within the familiarity of a place he called home for now.

When he stepped back into the living area, the room was no longer dark. The glow of a holographic projection spilled across the studio apartment, throwing shifting light over the walls. Sitting on the couch watching the hovering screen was Min, his human roommate.

Min was a skinny man in his early twenties, though his lined and scarred face gave him an older appearance. His shoulder-length, dark blue hair hung over the sides of his face loosely, and his dark eyes were locked in a daze while the late-night post-New-Year broadcast played on.

Raylen padded across the floor, unashamed of his nudity in front of the human. Min didn't look up or say anything as Raylen approached. He hesitated for only a moment, then hopped onto the couch beside Min, slowly sinking into the cushions.

For a moment, neither of them spoke. The broadcast's quiet audio filled the space, casting both man and lemur in ghostly blue light as the flickering images of live music acts, entertainment, and ads played before them.

"So... How'd it go tonight?" Min asked casually, not breaking eye contact with the screen.

Raylen leaned back on the couch, stretching his legs out and scratching at his bare crotch, his fur still faintly damp and fluffed from the shower.

"Not great," he replied in a similar casual voice.

Min turned his head just enough to glance at his naturalist lemur roommate, sitting unbothered beside him. "Yeah, well, it's the first. Don't forget you owe me rent."

Raylen sighed, getting up to reach for the discarded jacket crumpled on the floor by the bathroom, still soaked from the rain.

"Here," he said, returning to the couch with a stack of dakin cards presented to the human.

Min snatched the cards from his hand and started counting, lips moving silently as he thumbed through the stack. His face twisted as he eyed his smaller roommate with scrutiny.

"Come on, man! It's four hundred. You know that!" Min said with aggravation rising. "There's only two-sixty here."

"I know, and I'm sorry. It's been a slow month."

Min flipped through the cards like they were a playing deck, shaking his head. "Nah. You agreed to four hundred on the first of every month. You were late last month, and you're gonna be late again this month too? What the hell, man?!"

Raylen's ears flicked back as he raised his voice. "I'm not exactly made of money here, alright! I'm doing the best I can. What am I supposed to do?"

"Fuck, man," Min groaned as he leaned forward, rubbing his forehead. "You know I need the money! This was our arrangement! Remember? I let you stay here in this spacious government-supplied housing unit, where you, a sentient, aren't even allowed. I keep the cops off your ass, and in return, you pay me a generously discounted rent, so I can keep my artisan status and my citizenship, so *you* can continue living *here*. That was the deal, man."

Raylen tilted his head, a sly grin creeping onto his muzzle. "Don't forget I give you the companionship you so desperately need."

"Yeah, sure, whatever, man. I'm the one helping you out. Remember? I could easily kick your furry ass back to the curb where I found ya."

"You're not even discounting me that much. I could get a place for not much more down the street."

"Then go fuckin' move there then! I don't need you!"

Raylen folded his arms, tail flicking in irritation as he grumbled under his breath.

"Don't you forget I'm the one helping you. Remember?" Min added. "I coulda left you out there living in that fuckin' box. I took you in and gave you a place to eat, sleep, and shit. The least you could do is show some fucking gratitude and pay me what I'm expected."

Raylen snapped his head toward him. "Then why *did* you help me?!"

Min threw his hands up, chuckling a mix of annoyance and exhaustion. "I dunno! You needed a place to stay. I needed some extra cash. You know… Plus, I thought it'd be cool gettin' high n' shit with a talking lemur."

"Was it?"

Min blew raspberries and rolled his eyes. "Whatever, man."

"Look. I'll get you the money once I have it, alright? I just need like a couple more days with better tips."

"No."

Raylen blinked. "*No*?"

"I'll give you one more day. That's it."

"One day?! How am I supposed to make that much in one day?! I'm lucky if I even get close to fifty dakins in a night."

"I dunno what to tell you, man. Sell your body to some pervert sentos? Pawn off that guitar? I don't care. Figure it out!"

"I'm *not* selling my guitar! Are you *kidding*?! That's literally how I make my money."

Min shrugged. "Still got that first option then."

Raylen chuckled. "Yeah, and you'd be my first customer, wouldn't you?"

Min snorted. "Fuck you."

Raylen snickered as he stood up on the couch to reach over to the countertop of the kitchen. As he did, his tail instinctively lifted, giving Min a view he was not desiring.

"Dude." Min grimaced, putting his hand up to censor the image of the lemur's backside.

Raylen returned to his reclined position on the couch with a pipe in one hand and a small plastic bag in the other. Carefully, he filled the pipe with the grainy, gray substance from the bag, tamping it down lightly with a finger.

"How 'bout we just forget about money for now and celebrate the new year?" Raylen said as he worked. "Happy…fucking…new year, motherfucker."

Clamping the top closed, he placed the pipe to his lips and took a long draw. Instantly, the drug inside was vaporized and filled his lungs. Satisfied, he passed the pipe over to Min, who took it without reluctance, taking a strong hit of his own.

The drug took hold, wrapping them both in its altering effects. Raylen's body grew numb yet ultra-sensitive. His thoughts became as light as feathers as the room drifted around him. Together, they floated in that hazy space between consciousness and dreams as the night consumed them, forgetting their troubles for the time as the morning of the new day crept in.

The sunlight blasted into the small apartment like an uninvited guest, its rays striking Raylen directly in his closed eyes. The overwhelming orange through his eyelids forced him from his slumber as he groaned softly and stretched, protesting the notion of consciousness. Rolling over onto his belly on the couch, his tail twitched from side to side as he buried his face into the cushions.

For a few minutes, he lingered in that hazy space between dream and waking with a headache creeping into his sinuses. Eventually, the daylight and hangover took conquest over his body, preventing him from further sleep. Then, his eyes opened fully, and the haze shattered.

He sat up, still locked in groggy disorientation. As his eyes began to focus, he glanced around the room and noticed something unexpected. He blinked a few times to confirm what he was seeing.

The front door stood wide open.

Raylen jolted up. A chill ran through his fur. Something felt wrong about it all.

He sat up quickly, eyes darting around the small apartment. Nothing appeared ransacked or out of place. But the space where his guitar case should have been…was empty.

The realization hit him like a punch to the chest. His guitar—his only possession of real value, his livelihood, his companion—was missing.

He stumbled to his feet, heart pounding, and shot over to the open doorway. He looked out into the hallway and saw it was devoid of people. He slammed the door and frantically searched the apartment. Maybe he had put it somewhere else, he thought. Perhaps Min moved it before he left that morning and accidentally left the door open. He needed to know. He rummaged through every one of the few rooms within the tiny space. He searched Min's bed area and under it. Nothing. He even resorted to looking in the bathroom. It was not there.

For a moment, he could only stand there, breath quick and shallow, on the verge of a panic attack. Then, the undeniable reality came to light in his mind.

His guitar had been stolen.

CHAPTER 2

Panic consumed Raylen.

His pulse spiked as he tore through the tiny apartment, searching every corner. No sign of Min. No guitar. The reality of it hit him with nauseating force, exacerbating the hangover he was already experiencing. The guitar was everything to him. His only real possession of value, his only source of income, and the one piece of stability in a world that never stopped pushing him down was gone.

With a swipe of his hand, an augmented reality display materialized in his vision, displaying the familiar semi-transparent home screen user interface of his neurally-integrated com. Scrolling quickly through its screens, he found Min's contact and initiated a call.

CONNECTING… CALL ENDED.

Almost instantly, the call was declined. He tried again. The same thing.

"Come on, you fucking asshole, answer," he muttered under his breath, pacing in circles around the small living room. The call failed to connect a third time. His tail lashed behind him in growing agitation.

He sent a text message and waited. Minutes passed with it left unread. He then left a voice message, voice trembling with anger and confusion. "Min, call me back as soon as you get this! I'm not fuckin' around, man! This is serious! Someone stole our shit! Call me or get back over here now!"

Shutting off the AR display of his com, he sank onto the couch, hands rubbing furiously against his face. Everything felt like it was crumbling around him. He didn't know what to do. He couldn't call the marshals; they would just evict him from the apartment. Thoughts swirled in his head wildly like a chemical reaction ready to ignite. How could this happen?

Suddenly, something registered in his head. A small, sharp inconsistency.

He got up and looked around again, this time with deliberate focus. It didn't take long to notice what he'd missed before. The kitchen counter was still cluttered with appliances. Though cheap, some retained their value, such as the bright red blender that could have fetched an easy thirty to fifty dakins from a desperate addict looking for a quick fix; it was sitting right by the door, untouched. But the pipe and drugs were gone. The shelf in the bathroom with Min's toiletries—empty. Yet all of Raylen's things were still there. The stack of sketchbooks that always sat beside the couch was also gone. Min's old duffel bag and backpack, missing. So too were the boxes of art supplies, books, and even the trading card binders and adult paraphernalia he kept under his bed. Every trace of Min had vanished, and yet not a single item of Raylen's was gone, except for his guitar.

It was no coincidence. Sickness threatened to rise in his stomach as the realization dawned.

Min hadn't just left for the day. He had taken everything and abandoned Raylen while he peacefully slept. He stole from him.

The punch came before he could stop it. His fist slammed into the wall, cracking the beige surface beneath his knuckles. He stomped across the room, tail lashing violently and teeth bared, kicking the couch and tossing a small side table across the room, where it crashed into a corner.

"That asshole!" he shouted.

Min was a lazy opportunist who never wished to contribute to society in any meaningful way to guarantee his citizenship. So, he abused the system, utilizing its "artisan" loophole to avoid working and benefit from free housing, food, health care, and other basic needs. But in order for him to keep his artisan status, he needed to prove an income. That's where Raylen came into the picture. Min saw a chance to exploit a sentient in need and squeeze the money out of him. Raylen figured once Min realized he wasn't going to get the amount of money he desired, he'd move on to the next poor soul. Min was a leech, one who likely pawned his guitar for some extra cash.

Raylen stopped, breathing hard, trembling. He should've known better. He had trusted someone who saw him as nothing more than a convenience. But what choice had he really had? It was this or the streets, begging for shelter in a city that barely tolerated his kind.

Now there was nothing left. No real possessions. No means to earn a living. Just a pile of dirty clothes, an empty apartment, and a broken trust.

Raylen slammed the door behind him and stormed down the hallway. Once outside, he looked around. The city had the audacity to be beautiful. Blue skies stretched wide, painted by puffy white clouds drifting lazily past the high towers of glass surrounding him. The grass and trees in the park glistened in emerald while sunlight flashed off wet concrete like a thousand sparkling stars. A cool breeze graced the fur on his face. But he wasn't having any of it.

He cut across the rectangular front lawn of trampled grass and mud and began to pace. Back and forth. Tail lashing vehemently as he did. Seething words hissed through his teeth at no one and everything. He cursed at everything the new year had taken from him.

Across the street, two of the human gangsters posted near the bar turned to watch. One elbowed the other and pointed; both started laughing. Raylen didn't notice them. His own rage had taken priority of his focus.

He screamed in his feral voice and let himself fall backward into the wet grass. As the water seeped into his jacket, which was already dirty and smelly enough, he lay there for a long moment, staring up at the sky as the clouds shifted and reformed in slow, gentle metamorphoses. His yellowish eyes caught the sun and reflected it like fire. He breathed slowly, trying to calm himself. A slow, deep breath escaped his lungs, followed by another. The rhythm eventually evened out.

"Okay…okay…this sucks. This sucks a lot," he spoke quietly to himself. "We've been through worse, right? We can do this. Come on, you hume-modified brain, think this through… What are we gonna do?"

He closed his eyes. He listened to the wind rushing through the trees, the soft roar of the city from traffic flying overhead, and the whir of insects scattered about in their hidden places. When he opened them, he felt a sense of resolve return. He sat up and took a deep breath.

"We go for a walk. It's a nice day out, right? Let's just get some air and some fucking sunshine and go for a *lovely* fucking walk!"

He stood, brushing the loose grass and muck off his jacket, pants, and tail, then stepped off the lawn.

Raylen wandered without direction for nearly twenty minutes, the city wrapping itself around him. His anger had mostly cooled by now, replaced by a numbness that often followed many of the misfortunes of his youth. Ahead, the skyline of downtown Tokyo grew dense. Mile-tall towers climbed into the clouds, each one braced by bridges and massive platforms that linked them together like components of some enormous art piece. Above, the air shimmered with the ceaseless currents of autonomous flying vehicles weaving between structures.

Down here at the lowest level on the outskirts, the scale was more mundane. The narrow streets were lined with mid-rise buildings, overpasses for trains, and small shops. People drifted casually through the corridors of concrete, brick, and glass, carrying bags, drinks, or walking their non-sentient dogs. He was the only sentient among them, and the only one of his species in a sea of humanity. Most didn't even notice him or chose not to. Those who did shot glances before moving on, as though he were something of interest, but nothing unseen before.

He found a bench beneath a perfectly trimmed round tree and sat down for a respite. His fur rippled in a gust of wind as he leaned forward to stare blankly at the ground.

He needed a plan.

If Min were truly gone, then the apartment would soon be taken from him as well. Sooner or later, one of two things would happen. Either the property management would realize they had a non-authorized non-human squatter and have him removed by authorities, or the unit would be reassigned, and he would be locked out. One way or another, he faced being back on the streets, but he knew he had some time before anyone caught on.

He exhaled slowly and focused calmly. Living life, sleeping like a stray animal outside, was the last thing he wanted again, but he needed to figure out where to go. He'd first have to find a way to earn again. But without his guitar? That was like asking him to breathe underwater.

Neither Tokyo nor the empire of Aneti was kind to sentients when it came to honest work. Even the simplest jobs demanded citizenship, which he could never attain. Though jobs existed for sentients, there were few available, especially in this human-dominated city. Furthermore, securing employment would often take months, a luxury of time he couldn't afford. That was assuming anyone would hire a homeless sentient with no job experience beyond that of forced child labor in a disreputable circus.

He rolled over some ideas in his mind. Maybe he could sell drugs. Maybe join a sentient gang, like the Getazan or the Black Buredos of South Tokyo. No. The thought curdled his gut. He could never see himself walking down such dark paths, even as a desperate last resort.

Then, he thought about Min's comment from the night before. Prostitution. He snorted, shaking his head with a short, bitter laugh. Sure, he loved getting laid from time to time, but he'd sooner rob a bank than even consider such a livelihood.

Who was he kidding? He wasn't a criminal by nature; he was thrust into it out of need. Every time he'd stolen something, it had been for his own survival. Food from a convenience store, the clothes he was wearing from department store racks, and other needed things were all taken from corporations that would never truly feel the sting of loss. He had never wanted to hurt anyone. He had never taken from someone who couldn't afford to lose it. All he ever wanted was to live his own life in peace, far away from the abuses of humanity.

Still, he needed to do something, and soon. Playing guitar was the only thing he was ever good at. It was his life. He sorely wanted it back.

He leaned back on the bench and stared up through the gaps in the branches, looking up at the massive skyscrapers piercing the clouds. Somewhere in that endless sprawl, his guitar was out there, lost eternally.

Then, he saw it. It was not his guitar, but an opportunity.

Across the street, a white, windowless, trapezoidal-shaped van hovered in a narrow alley beside a small bar. Its back doors stood open, and several men were unloading music equipment: speaker stacks, mic stands, drum cases, and among them, a single, hard-shell guitar case. It gleamed under the sunlight as though spotlit by the heavens themselves.

For a long moment, Raylen just watched them. He hated himself for even considering the idea that crept into his brain. But necessity had a way of dulling guilt. He needed that guitar more than they did, and surely they could afford to buy another one. He *needed* it! This was his chance.

He rose from the bench and walked down the side of the street as if on a casual stroll. Once out of sight, he darted across the street and slipped into the shadows of the neighboring building, pressing himself against the cool concrete of the wall separating him from the alleyway. He peered around rapidly. No one else was around to see him. Even in broad daylight, it just might work, he thought.

Inching his way closer to the edge of the wall, he lowered himself to peek around. He could see straight down the alley, but his line of sight to the men unloading was obscured by the van. They were busily unpacking the last of the items from the back and chatting with one another in bursts of Japanese. He crouched lower, scanning his surroundings, piecing together a plan.

He looked up at the tree above him. It was tall with thick branches that arched over the alley from the neighboring property. The trunk wasn't far.

Raylen rushed over and placed a hand against the bark. Natural instincts activated as he began to climb. His muscles knew the rhythm before his mind did. In a few quick movements, he scaled the tree, gripping with both hands and feet-hands, tail adjusting his balance as he ascended.

He crawled along one of the sturdier branches until he was directly above the alley. From here, he had a much clearer view of the men below. There were four of them standing around, smoking and laughing as they talked, oblivious to the large, conspicuously-patterned primate directly overhead.

They spoke only Japanese, but he caught enough to understand most of it. He had only learned the language the prior year, so it was still tough for him. The tallest of the men gestured toward the bar and said something about grabbing a drink. Another replied, nodding his head and smiling.

The one nearest the side door began to follow, but the others stopped him, asking him to stay behind and watch the gear. He agreed reluctantly, though not before demanding they bring him back a beer.

The group continued their way around the corner into the front entrance, leaving the last man alone by the back door.

From his perch above, Raylen's eyes remained locked on the solitary musician below.

The man by the door seemed attentive at first, eyes scanning the alley like a proper guard. For a moment, Raylen thought he might stay that way until the others returned. Then, the man lifted a hand, making a small flicking motion in front of his face, indicating he was accessing his com. His gaze went vacant and unfocused as his hands and fingers made their motions.

Perfect.

The guitar case leaned against the wall just a few paces from the man. It was closer than he would've liked, but if he moved fast enough while the man was distracted by his games, there was a chance for success. His heartbeat sped up, but he steadied his breath. It was now or never.

He crouched low on the branch, tail flicking rapidly for balance, and jumped.

The impact on the van's roof resulted in a louder-than-expected metallic thud. The whole vehicle rocked briefly. Raylen froze, flattening himself against the cold metal and curling his tail around his body.

The man looked up and stood, squinting toward the van. His shoes scuffed against the pavement as he circled the van, peering around the alleyway to investigate. Making his way to the back, he looked upward at the tree branches swaying. Opening the back of the van, he gave it a quick inspection, then popped back out and closed the doors. Seeing nothing around, he gave a skeptical grunt and returned to his post.

Raylen held his breath and kept himself motionless. Seconds turned into minutes. The man settled back against the wall, hand returning to flicking through an invisible screen, attention once again buried in his private, virtual game.

Raylen dared a peek. The man hadn't moved. His eyes were glassy, fingers poking at the air.

Raylen studied his surroundings. Distances, obstacles, escape path, all of it he rehearsed through his mind several times. His pulse roared as adrenaline surged, but his mind stayed sharp. All he needed was one quick drop, grab the case, and bolt for the street.

He exhaled and leaped.

His feet hit the ground softly in a crouch. In the same motion, he snatched the guitar case, then ran.

The shout came soon after. "Oi!"

Footsteps clapped behind him. Raylen didn't look back; he didn't have to. He could hear the pursuit closing. But speed was something he had in his blood. His lighter body darted through the alley with the agility of a wild animal, leaping over precariously stacked drum parts.

He rounded the corner, only to skid to a stop.

The other three band members stood outside the bar, their faces transforming from surprise to fury in an instant once they saw the case in his hands.

"Shit," Raylen blurted, forcing himself out of his deer-in-the-headlights reaction to bolt the other way.

They shouted, voices overlapping, as the clamor of shoes increased in tempo with their sprint toward him. Raylen dashed down the street with everything he had in him, the heavy case banging against his side, threatening to free itself from his grip. It slowed him, and he could already feel his lungs and muscles straining. So, he resorted to what came natural by altering his human-like run into something more lemur-like. He bounded in short bursts while carrying the guitar case over his head, springing off his legs like his ancestors would, gaining valuable distance with each leap. It looked silly, but it bought him a safe gap from his pursuers. Sadly, his stamina was fading fast.

He reached the end of the street and cut hard around the corner, only to stumble into the unexpected. Three people on hover scooters zoomed straight for him. He jerked back instinctively to avoid the collision, lost his footing, and fell. The case slipped from his grasp, hitting the cement as he crashed back-first against a retaining wall.

He scrambled to recover it, but the footsteps slowing to a halt beside him told him he was out of time. The four men closed in, surrounding him in a tightening ring.

Raylen froze, chest heaving. He raised his hands slowly in surrender, ears flattening nervously. Maybe, he thought, just maybe they'd show mercy to a cute little lemur.

They did not.

One of the men snatched the guitar case from the ground while the other three closed in around him, their large bodies blotting out the sunlight behind them.

"Sent trash," one of them said in a thick accent before delivering a swift punch to the side of Raylen's muzzle.

They proceeded to beat him relentlessly in unison. After the first few punches, Raylen dropped to the ground, overwhelmed by their numbers. Boots connected with his ribs, his spine, and the soft flesh beneath his arms. He curled into a ball on the cold asphalt, arms wrapped over his head to protect himself. When the battering against his body finally ceased, a glob of warm saliva landed on his nose, sliding down the sides of his mouth as they left him trembling on the curb like discarded garbage.

Carefully picking himself up and wiping the human spit from his muzzle, he watched with humiliation as the four men walked casually away laughing, one of them carrying the guitar case.

CHAPTER 3

Defeated and disheveled, Raylen turned and limped down the street. His hands shook at his sides from adrenaline that hadn't quite faded. His ribs ached where one of them had kicked him especially hard, and every breath came with a sharp reminder of it. He brushed off the dirt from his jacket and pants, smearing it more than cleaning it. A faint wince crossed his face as he pressed a hand to his side. It felt tender, but not fractured. He knew the difference, as this was not his first beating. And maybe, he thought bitterly, it was one he'd deserved.

A part of him was relieved that he had failed. Replacing his stolen guitar by stealing another's would've only passed his misery along to someone else. The embarrassment of guilt overpowered his shame of losing the fight. He knew what he had done was wrong, but knowing that didn't alleviate his hardship. His burden remained on his shoulders, and no solution came to mind. Maybe this really was the end of the road. Perhaps his days from here on would be spent begging for scraps or scavenging like a feral animal.

Life carried on around him as if nothing had occurred. Humans drifted between shops and offices, chatting over meals, their lives seemingly so comfortably mundane. Overhead, holographic billboards veiled the sky and buildings with forced optimism. Endless ads played silently for new technology, off-world travel destinations, and expensive private vehicles. Each one carried with it a reminder of how far those luxuries were from his grasp. Through it all, he moved slowly, head hung low and tail dragging.

Something caught his eye. Just ahead, at the corner, was a wide display window for a large music store. He crossed the street and slowed to a stop. Behind the glass, rows of guitars hung in perfect order along the walls. Between them, keyboards, bassynths, eluniators, strings, brass, amplifiers, and drum kits stood amongst shelves and displays full of digital processors and other professional audio equipment. It was all there waiting to be explored. He stood there for a long moment, staring in wonder, the reflection of his tired face merging with the instruments behind the glass.

The thought crept in uninvited once again. He quickly shook his head. *No. Don't do it,* he thought. *They have better security and surveillance. It's not worth the jail time.*

Still, his feet carried him closer to the front entrance. He wanted to look, just to feel something familiar again, and have a momentary distraction from a bad day. So, he pushed through the door.

Before he could take more than two steps inside, a man in a uniform intercepted him.

"No! No animals! No sentens," the man said sternly, motioning for Raylen to walk back through the doors.

Raylen paused, eyes glancing between the plethora of musical instruments and the man blocking his path with crossed arms. Then, without argument, he turned and stepped back out onto the curb.

He stood there a moment, staring at the reflection of the amber-eyed, furred primate dressed in stained clothing in the darkened glass. Then, he shook his head and turned away.

He didn't make it far before the weight of it all finally caught up with him. His knees gave out, and he slid back against a wall. Burying his face in his arms and wrapping his long tail around himself, he tried his hardest to hold back the tears.

The sound of laughter drifted from the music store's doorway as a couple of women and one man with long dark hair reminiscent of a classic rock star—each of them carrying youthful beauty—stepped out into the sunlight. The man and his girlfriend walked ahead, carrying a glossy bag and chitchatting, while the other carried herself with slow confidence. She had short blonde hair, sunglasses, and was dressed in all black, from a designer jacket to her fashionable boots.

The couple was halfway down the street when she stopped dead in her tracks. Her gaze had caught on the small figure sitting against the wall. Her friends ahead noticed too and paused briefly to point, smile, and gave a sympathetic "Aww! So cute!" before continuing their trek. She, however, stayed behind, studying him.

"Hey! You coming?!" the man called back.

"Go on! I'll meet you there!" she replied in an elegant British accent as she waved them off.

She turned back to Raylen and approached slowly. Crouching down, her expression softened as she peered at him over the edge of her sunglasses.

"Hi there. Are you okay?" she asked, as though speaking to a young child.

Raylen lifted his head, eyes tired. "Oh…I've had worse days."

His distinctly masculine voice caught her off guard. She blinked, realization dawning that the lemur was an adult sentient.

"Sorry, I've…never seen a sentient like you before," she said, removing her sunglasses. "You're very cute. You're a lemur, right?"

"Yeah. Look," he said wearily. "I appreciate it, but I'm not really in the mood right now. I'd like to be left alone, please."

She rose to her feet, arms crossing as she glanced toward the store, thinking. "That was you trying to get into the store just now, wasn't it?"

Raylen followed her gaze, then sighed. "Yeah. I was just… I dunno what I was thinking. Not like I can afford anything in there anyway. I'm just an idiot."

"You're not an idiot. It just sounds like you're on some hard times, is all. It will get better."

"Will it?" he asked aggressively as he looked up at her.

The question remained unanswered as silence followed.

She hesitated, then tilted her head. "So, do you play an instrument?"

"I did…until my guitar got stolen. Was the only thing I had," he replied, waving his hand dismissively.

"I'm terribly sorry to hear that." She crouched again, meeting his eyes. "Were you any good?"

"At guitar? Yeah, I guess. I mean, that's how I make a living… Used to, anyway."

"Mhm," she mumbled, then glanced over at the entrance. "Tell you what. How about I escort you in? I know the manager. I'm certain he'll make an exception to allow you inside if I'm there. Are you interested?"

"You'd do that?"

She nodded.

"Okay. Yeah. Why not?" His tone carried disbelief more than agreement.

"But…you must promise not to steal or damage anything, okay?"

He gave a small, incredulous laugh. "Come on, what do you take me for?"

She gave him a long, scrutinizing look.

Raylen groaned and stood up. "Yeah, sure, okay. Promise."

That earned him a smile. She nodded once.

"Wait here."

He watched her turn and stride back toward the music store, the sunlight catching in her flawless, golden hair. The scent of her perfume lingered lightly in the air. It was pleasant, like vanilla, and it gave him a sudden sense of ease, but he couldn't pinpoint why.

Raylen waited on the curb, fidgeting and occasionally checking his com for new posts on various media streams. Minutes dragged. But then the door opened again, and she stepped out with a smile and waved him over.

He hesitated only a moment before crossing the threshold. Inside, the store was a cathedral of music. Rows upon rows of instruments lay suspended on illuminated walls. Guitars gleamed like relics, their curves catching the light in every color. Their chrome, gold, and other anodized metal hardware sparkled, each one seeming to cry out to be held. Every surface had something to see and explore, and for Raylen, this was akin to a toy store in a childhood he never had.

Raylen followed her slowly, eyes wide, scanning the displays as they walked through the aisles. He stopped now and then to point out instruments, such as custom models and aged vintage pieces with price tags that made him cringe. These were guitars he could only dream about—instruments from the worlds of the rich and famous he'd never be allowed to enter.

"You said you play guitar, right? Would you like to try one of them out?" she asked.

He looked up at her, caught off guard by her offer. His gaze drifted over the wall again until it locked once again on a seven-string hanging higher than the rest he had admired earlier. The body shimmered with a metallic teal finish that seemed to shift color depending on the angle of the light. It was beautiful. It was flawless. And it was expensive.

"You like that one?" she asked, pointing directly at it.

"Yeah, but it's too much. I don't wanna—"

Before he could finish, she turned to a nearby employee across the way and spoke rapid Japanese. The man looked hesitant at first, but replied politely. They went back and forth for a few seconds until he finally nodded, bowed slightly, and made his way from behind the counter. Grabbing a ladder, he reached up to take the guitar from its mount. Returning, he reluctantly handed it down to Raylen, as though presenting a sacred artifact.

Raylen accepted it carefully, holding it as if it were made of precious china. The finish caught the overhead light, and he gazed at how the paint shifted the color ever so slightly from a bright teal to a deep azure. He ran his fingers gently along the body, tracing every contour, then brushed them over the blackened knobs and pickups. The fretboard held a vine-like design of blue pearloid inlays, crafted only by the most artistic among luthiers. When he touched the strings, they resonated faintly beneath his fingertips as he slid across them. This truly was an instrument begging to sing.

He stood there for a long moment just admiring it. Then, he found a nearby amp sufficient for a test drive. Once he was wirelessly connected, he checked his tuning and adjusted the controls until the tone sounded just right at a low volume. A deep breath. A soft strum of a small chord. It required only the lightest of touches to elicit a sound that was liquid candy to his ears.

Defiantly, he turned the volume up.

The first chord rang through the store like thunder. Heads instantly turned, startled by the blaring sound. Normally, anyone would have been shut down for committing such an act, but then his fingers came to life. He tore through scales, tapping and sliding, his feet-hand joining in to hammer complex, multi-stringed arpeggios while his hands transitioned between impossible chords and inhuman legatos. In seconds, the quiet store transformed into a stage.

He climbed atop a stool, then a speaker cabinet, still playing, stringing together unthinkable runs. He further boasted his skills by segueing into playing upside down, backward, and over his head. His movements remained effortless and impeccable. Eyes half-closed in focus, he lost himself in the moment. More customers moved closer to watch, some capturing every second with their coms.

He finished with a screaming bent note at the highest possible fret, then dropped it down to one final ringing power chord before killing the volume. The room erupted. Applause, commentary, cheers. A few people even approached to pat him on the back or ruffle his head fur, drowning him in compliments. Raylen couldn't stop smiling. It felt good to hear the applause once again.

But it would surely be but a temporary moment of satisfaction. He turned to hand the guitar back to the woman, but she waved him off.

He looked at her questioningly.

"That was impressive! Seeing what you can do with that, you two deserve each other," she said, smiling.

"It's twenty-seven hundred dakins. I can't afford—"

"I'm buying it. It's yours."

Raylen's eyes widened. "What?!"

They stepped out of the music store into the warm afternoon light with Raylen carrying a brand-new guitar case in one hand and a small travel-sized combo amp in the other. They both paused by the front entrance. For a long moment, he simply stood there, staring in disbelief at his prizes, as though afraid they might vanish if he blinked. The events of the last hour felt surreal.

"There must be something I can do to repay you for this," Raylen said quietly, glancing back up at her.

She adjusted her sunglasses and smiled, the reflection of the midday sunlight flickering across the dark lenses.

"No need. I believe you're going places, Raylen. I really do! And you're going to need to have the right instruments to get to where you need to be."

"But this is a lot of money."

"Oh, money is of little concern to a payan's daughter," she said, dropping her sunglasses to give him a wink. "Unlike most of the other spoiled, rich arseholes in this world, I'd prefer to see money go to those who truly need and deserve it."

He kept his gaze on her, still overwhelmed. "I mean…I'm grateful. I'm *more* than grateful! Please don't get me wrong here. But why me? Of all the bums in this city, why me?"

She grinned. "Well, I suppose I have a soft spot for lemurs. What can I say? You're bloody adorable!"

He smiled in return as she reached out to give him a gentle pet on the head, then looked back down at his guitar, still in disbelief.

"Well, glad someone around here likes me," he said.

"By the way, I don't mean to be presumptuous, but…do you have some place to keep yourself and that guitar safe and dry?"

"I mean…maybe for a few more days until the cops kick me out of my current place. But, I'll figure something out."

Without hesitation, she pulled a small stack of dakin cards from her pocket and handed them to him.

"What are you doing? No," Raylen protested.

"Take it," she said. "It should hold you over for a while. But, please don't waste it all away. That's all I ask."

He froze, staring at the stack of hundreds in disbelief. "Are you serious right now?"

As he took the money, he began blinking rapidly to fend off the tears that threatened to spill over.

"I'd offer to let you stay with me, but my reputation amongst my family would be tarnished if they found out, I'm sorry to say. That's the best I can offer you with what I have on me. I hope it'll be enough."

"You kidding? No, this is… This is more than enough. I can't… I can't begin to thank you enough. I-I don't know—"

She crouched down and hushed him with a soft gesture of her finger, then gave him a tender pet and a soft kiss on his muzzle.

"Just keep moving forward," she whispered, looking him in the eyes. "And don't ever give up the music. Promise me that. You have something special."

She stood, the sun haloing her figure as she glanced down the street.

"I'm afraid I must rejoin my friends before they drink all the wine without me. It was lovely meeting you, Raylen. Be well."

She turned and began walking away with the same slow, confident stride.

"Hold on!" he called out. She paused and looked back. "What-what was your name?"

"Emma." She smiled brightly once more before continuing down the street.

Raylen stood there, staring at her until she disappeared. He would never see her again, but he would never forget how one stranger with the means to help another could change a life forever.

He looked down at the guitar case in his hands with a wide grin on his face.

"Emma," he murmured to himself.

CHAPTER 4

Weeks passed.

Raylen had returned to the city's downtown center, where towers pierced the night sky and the air shimmered with the colors of neon accent lighting and holographic animations. But this time, it was different.

Armed with his new electric 7-string, his music now dominated the streets. The small amp beside him, though modest in size, provided a sufficient tone and loudness. When he strummed those first chords each evening, the sound carried far, cutting through the noise of the streets and turning heads. People finally noticed.

The money Emma had given him also helped cover at least a month's worth of rent at a cheap dormitory on one of the lower city levels. The place was smaller than Min's place and crowded with shared bathrooms and showers. But it was a roof, a bed, and most importantly, it had running hot water. After what he'd lived through, it was more than enough.

Still, he knew the financial assistance wouldn't last forever, and he needed to keep hustling to make ends meet. Five hundred sixty dakins a month wasn't much by most standards, but to him, it was a steep debt to pay. If he couldn't keep up, he'd be back to sleeping in the rain and cold.

So, he played. Every night, from afternoon until midnight or later, he played.

Crowds began to grow each night, gathering around him at his usual corner at the plaza's edge. The amplified sound, combined with his sharpened skills, attracted attention from blocks away. Commuters inevitably slowed their steps to watch, drawn in by both the intricate melodies that spilled from his fingers and the visual spectacle he offered. As the days passed, he had learned how to tap into the energy of the audience to keep them watching and wanting more.

He didn't sit in one spot anymore. No. He ran around like a child hopped up on sugar. He climbed on his stool and other nearby objects, balancing precariously as he played with three hands. He swung his guitar around, he threw it in the air and caught it, and he did any possible stunt he could think of, without missing a note or a beat. The crowd went wild every time.

Dakin cards rained into his case. Applause, whistles, and cheers often filled the air.

By the end of each night, Raylen's body ached, but seeing the red velvet fabric inside his case obscured by copious scatterings of cash made it all worth it. Double, sometimes triple, what he used to earn became a near-nightly occurrence. It was just enough to cover rent. Enough to eat. Enough to sleep a little more restfully each night.

Today, the night air on the upper plaza was crisp and chilly. There was not a cloud in the sky that evening, and the steady, gentle breeze helped cool Raylen as he performed. So far, it was turning out to be an average night with a modest crowd.

As always, Raylen was in his element, looping through his daily routine. Solos tore through the air, and fingers blazed across the fretboard. Each note rang sharp and clear. Around him, three dozen stood witnessing his small production. When he played recognizable classics and modern rock anthems, they cheered louder.

Far across the plaza, the old man stood clutching his electric violin, bowing along to his recording. His face was set in the same grim scowl upon seeing the crowds drawn to the lemur commanding the opposite corner. No one stopped to listen to him anymore. People passed him without a glance. Still, the man played on, swaying to his illusion of music, hopeful his con might earn him a dakin.

Raylen ended his set with a long, soaring bend that lingered and cut through the air like a battle scream, then followed it with a swift sweep of a low power chord, which faded into the applause that followed.

He grinned, breathing hard, and gave a conclusive bow.

Dakin cards poured into his open case as the crowd gradually thinned. Some waved as they left, others stayed behind to say a few words, but eventually the plaza quieted again, the echoes of his performance fading once more into the city's ambient background noise.

Raylen crouched down and began to count his tips, sorting through the pile rapidly. It was a little less than normal, but it would suffice. Rent was secured at least for the following month.

He suddenly sensed a presence approaching.

Quickly shuffling the money into his jacket pocket, he looked over. Just inches from him were a pair of polished black shoes. They looked expensive and were immaculately clean.

"Mou ikkyoku da," the man ordered.

Raylen sighed, trying to translate quickly and arrange the words correctly in his mind. "Gomen, mou…owari," he spoke awkwardly.

"Your Japanese is terrible. Do you speak Anetian better?" the man asked with a surprisingly smooth and fluent tone, completely devoid of any Japanese accent.

Raylen glanced upward, eyes meeting the polished black shoes again before following them to their owner. The Japanese man standing before him looked young. He couldn't have been much older than his mid-twenties. His black, fluffy hair was neatly styled, and his dark gray suit looked custom-fitted, trimmed with faint green accents. Everything about him radiated composure and wealth.

Raylen assumed he was another late-night local.

"I do," Raylen replied. "But, like I said, I'm wrapping up for the night."

"No. You're not," the man insisted. "You're playing one more song for me."

Raylen groaned quietly, realizing quickly the kind of heckler he'd need to deal with. As he locked the guitar case, he prepared to tell the stranger off.

"Look, man. I'm tired, and I just want to go home. I'll be here again tomorrow ni—"

That's when he looked up to see it. Protruding from the man's hand was the unmistakable gold and blue of a hundred-dakin card.

It took him little time to change his mind and reverse course. Quickly, he pulled his guitar back out of its case.

"Alright, one more song it is!" Raylen said as he set things up again. "But that's it, okay?"

The man stepped back, arms folded, patient and still as a statue, while Raylen reconnected the amp and slung the strap over his shoulder.

"So, uh, do you have a request?"

"Play me your best work. Impress me," the man said calmly.

Raylen tilted his head, eyebrow raised. "Impress you, huh?..." He thought for a moment, then nodded. "Alright."

He began to play.

What emerged from the speaker was intricate, yet melodic. It was an instrumental piece originally written and performed by Leo Friedman, a famous guitar virtuoso from the decade prior. The song was one few guitarists dared attempt, let alone come close to mastering. But Raylen glided through it effortlessly. Even in the section known for its notorious difficulty, he did not miss a note.

Pedestrians stopped, recognizing both the song and the talent. A small crowd reformed, drawn once again to the sentient who played like a man who'd signed his soul away at the crossroads.

When the final note faded, the few that remained applauded. All, except for the man in the gray suit. He remained cross-armed, face impassive.

Raylen looked at him, waiting. The man eventually moved. To Raylen's dismay, he took the hundred-dakin card and placed it back in his jacket pocket.

"Hey, man, what the hell?! You said—"

"Stop!" the man shouted assertively.

Raylen froze, eyes narrowing.

"What I just saw," he began slowly, "does not deserve a hundred dakins..." He let a pause stretch long before continuing his thought. "...It deserves more. Put your things away and follow me."

"Hey, hold on," Raylen said, standing defiantly. "What the hell is this? You're not some weird hume trying to coerce me back to your place for some freaky shit, are you? I played you your fucking song. The least you can—"

"I *said*," the man interrupted in his assertive voice, "put your things away and follow me."

Raylen recognized it was an order from a human, which he legally could not refuse, and sighed nervously. "Why?"

The stranger reached into his inner jacket pocket and produced a business card. He handed it to Raylen with both hands.

Raylen took it carefully, mirroring the gesture, as was traditional. His eyes scanned the card, admiring the shimmer of metallic blue and the embossed, opalescent white ink that graced its surface. The name that was printed displayed Yokota Masayuki, Senior Talent Manager, JRM. The JRM logo was printed large and well-known worldwide.

Raylen's eyes widened. "The hell is this?"

"As I said, your skills do not owe you a mere hundred dakins. I believe you should see more than that. And you most certainly should not be performing out here like some vagrant. So, if you're interested, I have a lucrative opportunity I would like to present to you, but we must discuss it elsewhere. So…if you're interested, please follow me. If not, then I'll be on my way."

Raylen stared at the card in disbelief. His mind was locked, dumbfounded, and trying its best to process what he was seeing and hearing. Was this real?

"Okay then," Yokota said as he turned to leave after not receiving a response.

"Ho-ho-hold up!" Raylen scrambled.

He fumbled as he hurried to pack his guitar away and grab his things. Picking up the guitar case in one hand and the amp in the other, he rushed to catch up as the man strode toward the far end of the plaza.

"Okay, you've got my interest," Raylen said, winded as he struggled to meet Yokota's stride while awkwardly carrying his gear. "What's this about?"

Yokota did not respond right away as they walked side by side.

"That's quite the guitar you have there," Yokota said. "You must make pretty good tips to afford such a gem."

"Yeah, a friend bought it for me as a gift. So, what—"

"That was generous of them. I'm not much of a classical electric guy myself, but that particular model is quite stunning."

"Thanks, but I'd like to—"

"Here we are." Yokota stopped abruptly.

Raylen paused to notice a silver-and-blue private transport with black-tinted windows descending slowly and silently before them. Once settled, stationary inches above the concrete, the scissor door lifted open, revealing a plush, blue-lit interior.

Yokota turned to Raylen and motioned him inside. "If my new lemur friend would please step into my office."

Raylen hesitated. "Where are we going?"

"Nowhere, for now. This will give us some privacy to talk. Please," he said, gesturing again. "I promise nothing weird."

Reluctantly, Raylen stepped forward, only for Yokota to halt him with a raised hand.

"Hold on. I nearly forgot. Before you go any further, I need you to sign this."

A glowing holographic projection materialized between them, which appeared to be a short contract.

"What's this?" Raylen asked, squinting at it.

"NDA and promissory note. Standard practice in this industry. It's harmless, I assure you. It just says you won't disclose anything we talk about to anyone, and other legal bullshit you don't need to concern yourself with right now. It's not a record deal or anything of the sort."

Raylen rapidly skimmed the text briefly. Then, with a small shrug, he squiggled his signature in the highlighted box at the bottom. The hologram rapidly dissolved.

"Thank you, sir. You may now come on in," Yokota said, allowing Raylen to enter first and secure his belongings.

Inside, the vehicle was immaculate. The black leather seats, preheated with built-in warmers, embraced Raylen's chilled posterior. Ambient blue lighting along the panels provided a calming atmosphere that was just bright enough to illuminate the cabin. And the faint scent of cedar graced his nostrils with a sense of welcoming comfort. The door sealed beside them, muting the outside world completely.

They sat across from one another in brief silence.

"Let's get to it," Yokota finally said. "Recently, one of my clients expressed a strong interest in you and sent me out here to find you. They would like to audition you to be part of their act. Now, to be clear: they are not an arena-headlining act, but I believe they have what it takes to get there if we add a little spice to their mix. That's where you would come in. Now, ultimately, the decision rests in their hands whether they want to hire you or not, so I make no promises. But what I can tell you is, if it works out, you'd be looking at joining a three-record deal with global and interstellar tours, media features, and endorsements. This would include a meager low to mid-six-figure allowance up front, but in time, depending on sales, I believe we can get that number into the millions. I think this would be a—"

Raylen's eyes went wide.

"*Meager six figures*?! *Millions*?!" Raylen exclaimed, interrupting the man. "Are you for… I… H-*how*?! Why me? How do you even know me? And-and who?"

"A video was posted of you weeks back playing guitar in a music store. It's gotten a lot of views. You weren't aware?"

"No, I…" Raylen rubbed his face, dazed. "I can't believe this. I'm dreaming right now, right? This is a dream, and I'm going to wake up, and all this will be… You can't be serious! Shit. This is a prank, isn't it?"

"I am dead serious. Tell me, uh, Mr.…." The man motioned with his hand.

"Raylen. Just…Raylen."

"Tell me, Raylen. Would you be interested in auditioning as lead guitarist for an up-and-coming headlining band?"

"I mean, yeah, I would! But who are they? Do I know them?"

"Have you heard of Frontstrike?" he asked while jotting something into his com.

"Frontstrike? Not sure. Maybe? Sounds familiar."

"How much time will you need to learn their songs?"

"I dunno… Depending on complexity, maybe a day or two?"

"Great! Learn the songs. I've scheduled you for a trip to Jakarta this coming Saturday, where you'll audition for them in person at their private studio. Meet me here Saturday morning at eight sharp. Don't be late, okay? I'll send the invite to your com. Oh, and pack for warm weather." He gave Raylen a warm smile. "If all goes well, your days of street performing are about to shift to a much larger audience."

BE SURE TO CHECK OUT
THE NOVEL SERIES

SENTIENTS

WITH THE FIRST BOOK

SENTIENTS

Volume 1

Unite

Find out more at
emptyset-art.com/sentients

APPENDIX

THE NATION OF ANETI

A BRIEF HISTORY OF ANETI

Civilization collapsed. Societies crumbled, and nations fell as nuclear war devastated entire regions, reducing cities to ash. Whole continents became uninhabitable wastelands, scorched by radiation and stripped of life. Humanity teetered on the brink of extinction, its population plummeting to a mere few million scattered across the globe. In the wake of such catastrophic destruction, technology was lost, rendered useless in a world where power grids and communication systems no longer existed. Entire libraries of recorded history, stored on fragile digital systems, were wiped clean, leaving much of the past a mystery to the survivors.

Those who remained were few, clinging to existence in isolated pockets of the world. Amidst the wreckage, a resilient group of survivors in Australia began the slow and arduous process of rebuilding. They scavenged what they could from the remnants of the old world—tools, knowledge, scraps of technology—piecing together a fragile semblance of society. What began as a desperate struggle to survive eventually grew into something more: a community, then a nation, united by a shared will to endure. After several generations, this fledgling society would one day give rise to the empire of Aneti.

For centuries, Aneti's power expanded through relentless wars and treaties, steadily growing until it held dominion over vast swaths of the Earth. What had started as a small coalition of survivors transformed into a dominating global force. The socialist democratic republic of Aneti established itself as the world's leading power, absorbing nations and erasing borders. Only a handful of independent countries remained, and even they struggled to resist Aneti's ever-encroaching influence. In its quest to mark a new era and sever ties with the broken world of the past, Aneti reset the global calendar, abandoning the Gregorian system and establishing the year "A" as the beginning of a new epoch.

Over the next five hundred years thereafter, the world saw an era of unprecedented transformation. With peace came the revival of scientific inquiry, leading to breakthroughs that once seemed unimaginable. Aneti's rise introduced technological revolutions, reshaping society in ways that even the old world could never have predicted. Among the greatest and most controversial of these advancements was the emergence of the sentients. Genetically and neurologically enhanced to possess human-like intelligence, these uplifted animals would usher in a new age in which the boundaries between species blurred and the definition of sapient life itself was rewritten.

POLITICS & ECONOMY

Aneti is a democratic republic with a socialist-capitalist economy.

Though all people are deemed equal under the Constitution, an individual cannot attain citizenship status without meeting the following requirements:

- Be human.
- Be a legally recognized adult (automatically designated at age 18).
- Fulfill at least one of the following conditions:
  - Be employed full-time (minimum 30 hours per week) or part-time if combined with another qualifying condition.
  - Serve as a recruited or active-duty military member.
  - Be enrolled in a nationally recognized educational institution (limited to seven years, unless extended by the institution).

- Hold elected office.
- Qualify as an "Artisan"—a broad exemption covering business owners, freelance artists, non-profit leaders, investors, and many others.
- Receive a special legal exemption (e.g., people with disabilities).

Failure to maintain these requirements may result in demotion to civilian status and/or legal penalties, which can include imprisonment, mandatory labor, or exile to wilderness regions, which are provisioned areas of Aneti beyond formal legal jurisdiction and organized society.

Benefits of citizenship under Aneti's socialized economy include:

- A guaranteed minimum wage, determined by job classification through the Department of Labor Services.
- Access to basic healthcare.
- Basic housing assistance if needed—typically co-ops or dormitories for single individuals, and small apartments for families.
- Provision of basic food and water if required.
- One week of paid time off per year, at the citizen's discretion.
- Basic retirement income after fifty years of citizenship.

While Aneti's socio-economic system guarantees basic provisions for its citizens, it also offers a path for social advancement through a structured class system. Citizens can meet their fundamental needs at the base level, but by rising in rank, they gain access to additional benefits and privileges. There are four more levels of citizenship a person may attain:

Honored Citizen

This tier consists of individuals who stand above the average citizen, including:

- Company managers
- Doctors, lawyers, engineers, scientists, and other elite professionals as designated by the Department of Labor Services
- Military personnel with a rank above private

- Wealthy artisans
- Low-level elected officials, such as mayors and judges
- Citizens recognized with national awards

Dignitary

The elite class comprised of individuals such as:

- Upper management or corporate executives
- Military officers
- Highly wealthy artisans
- Mid-level elected officials, such as congresspersons and governors
- Citizens honored with prestigious national awards

Payan

This class represents the wealthiest and most influential members of society, including:

- Company owners, presidents, and chief executives
- Military personnel holding ranks above Exultanein or serving in the Kometai Elite special forces
- Individuals with a net worth of ten million dakins or more (adjusted annually by the Department of Commerce)
- High-level elected officials, such as Senators and High Court justices
- Citizens granted this honorary rank directly by the Chancellor

Leader

Same as the Payan class, except members hold positions within the Grand Magistrate, serve as the Chancellor, or act as the Supreme General of the military.

Aneti's official currency is the **dakin**, denoted by the symbol **Đ**, which precedes the amount. It is an internally regulated currency, maintained and valued solely by the Anetian government, with minimal influence from foreign trade or external economic factors.

Primarily exchanged through non-physical, digital transactions, dakins can also be transferred using physical, plastic-like cards, which are about the length of a credit card but three-quarters as wide. These cards hold only whole values, with any fractional amounts always rounded up. Each dakin card can be quickly identified by its distinct color.

Đ1 silver with black print

Đ2 black with white print

Đ5 gold with black print

Đ10 burnt orange with black print

Đ15 bright magenta with black print

Đ20 violet with gold print

Đ25 green with gold print

Đ30 teal with gold print

Đ50 red with gold print

Đ100 blue with gold print

HISTORY OF THE SENTIENTS

The Early Discoveries (512–530 A)

In the year 512 A, a neurologist named Dr. Amari Kantu embarked on a groundbreaking project that would forever alter the course of history. His initial research aimed to cure a specific type of degenerative brain disease through neural interfacing, a technique that sought to remap neurons and create strategic connections to bypass the affected areas of the brain. In theory, the concept seemed viable. However, when Dr. Kantu began experimenting with lab animals, the process proved ineffective in combating the disease. While the results were disappointing, something unexpected caught his attention: several of the lab animals began to exhibit signs of advanced intelligence shortly before their sudden deaths. They even demonstrated the ability to mimic rudimentary speech.

The unanticipated side effect, while tragic, prompted Kantu to shift the focus of his research toward understanding the phenomenon of artificially enhanced intelligence. The potential of this discovery was undeniable. By sheer accident, Kantu had stumbled upon a method that could increase cognitive function in non-human animals, pushing them beyond their natural mental capacities.

For the next two years, Kantu's work faced significant challenges. His lab was eventually forced to shut down in 514 A when his funding was revoked due to the high mortality rate among the test subjects and the perceived lack of practical results. Hundreds of animals had died as a result of his experiments, and his reputation within the scientific community suffered. But Kantu was not one to give up easily.

Undeterred by his setbacks, he continued his research in private, relying on AI simulations to refine his theories while actively seeking new investors.

By 516 A, Kantu made a significant breakthrough. Through extensive modeling, he theorized that the uplift procedure could be stabilized if applied at the earliest stages of development. His research suggested that the ideal candidates were fetuses between the second and third trimesters, where the brain was still in the critical stages of formation. Post-birth procedures within the first two months of life were also possible but carried a much higher risk of failure. The key, Kantu realized, was to introduce the neural mapping early enough to integrate with the natural growth of the brain, allowing the cognitive enhancement to develop organically.

In 517 A, after publishing his theoretical research, Dr. Kantu attracted the attention of the University of Sydney's Marine Research Lab, a facility known for its pioneering work in marine biology. The lab agreed to partner with Kantu and allow him to perform his controversial procedure on one of their pregnant dolphins on the condition that, if the experiment failed, his career and funding would be permanently cut off. It was a high-stakes gamble, but Kantu took the risk, confident in his research. The result was Tesla, the first dolphin successfully uplifted, born with enhanced cognitive abilities far beyond those of any known Earthbound non-human species.

Tesla's existence would soon change the course of history. In 518 A, Tesla uttered his first word, sending shockwaves through the scientific community and capturing the attention of the global public. Kantu's breakthrough was no longer theoretical; it was real, tangible, and undeniable. The once-ridiculed neurologist was suddenly a figure of global fame. Funding poured into Kantu Labs, which became the first of many research facilities dedicated to the development, study, and nurturing of sentient animals, or sentients as they came to be known.

The following decade saw the expansion of Kantu's work on a massive scale. In 519 A, the first sentient chimpanzee was born, followed by several other species: lar gibbons, spider monkeys, orangutans, baboons, macaques, pigs, rats, dogs, cats, bonobos, and corvids. Each of these species exhibited enhanced cognitive abilities, capable of learning language, reasoning, and complex problem-solving. Kantu Labs soon became a bustling hub, with hundreds of sentient juveniles raised and educated side by side. The labs carefully managed their socialization, ensuring that sentients from predator and prey species could cohabitate peacefully. Fortunately, preexisting lab-grown meat technology, as well as the common conveniences of store-bought foods, eliminated the need for carnivorous species to consume their sentient prey counterparts, enabling the potential for harmonious coexistence.

As the years passed, Kantu's research deepened the world's understanding of uplift procedures. Some species, such as reptiles and amphibians, proved resistant to the enhancement, while others thrived under the process. Kantu's work never ceased, always exploring which creatures could join the ranks of the sapient. The implications for the future were staggering, as the young sentients would one day integrate into human society.

In the years that followed, Kantu Labs shifted focus toward bio-cybernetic and genetic enhancements, designed to help sentients adapt to a world built for humans. For species with physical limitations, the labs developed prosthetics, including cybernetic limbs and tools controlled via wireless neural interfaces. Many sentients were also genetically modified to walk upright, mimicking human bipedalism, while others were granted opposable thumbs to interact more easily with human-designed objects. Furthermore, lifespan enhancements and growth modifications were implemented, allowing smaller or short-lived species to mature and develop at rates comparable to humans, ensuring they had equal opportunities to learn, work, and thrive alongside their human counterparts.

The Sentient Expansion (530–540 A)

By the year 530 A, the world was captivated by the appearance of sentients. For the first time in history, the concept of intelligent, speaking creatures had departed the realm of fiction and become a reality. The notion of holding conversations with beings that had once been silent companions enthralled the public, and the fascination spread like wildfire. It wasn't just the novelty of speech that caught the public's attention—it was the realization that these sentients were fully self-aware, capable of complex thought, reasoning, and emotional depth.

People couldn't get enough of it.

By this time, Kantu Labs housed hundreds of sentient younglings across a wide variety of species. What had started with dolphins and chimpanzees had now expanded to include more apes, stoats, equines, and several other newly uplifted species. The lab continued its ambitious program of uplifting, further exploring the vast frontier of transcending what was once considered lower life.

To capitalize on growing public interest, Kantu Labs began offering guided tours and exhibitions, opening its doors to the curious masses. The reception was overwhelming. Visitors from all parts of the Anetian empire traveled far to see these extraordinary creatures up close, eager to behold the marvel of uplifting for themselves. Tens of thousands of people flooded the lab's exhibitions by the month, driving the funding Kantu needed to continue operations. It not only provided an opportunity for financial support but also fed into people's fascinations and allowed an opportunity for education and human interaction with the growing sentients.

For a time, it seemed as though the world had entered a new golden age of human-animal coexistence. The sentients flourished under the supervision of Kantu and his team—learning, maturing, and adapting to life alongside all other species of sentients and humans alike. There were no major incidents, no displays of uncontrolled aggression or instinct-driven behavior. They were civil, peaceful, and eager to understand the world they had been born into. Their relationships with one another were defined solely by curiosity and mutual respect.

But beneath the surface of the apparent harmony, a growing problem began to emerge. One that would soon prove impossible to ignore. As the eldest sentients matured, they began to experience a desire for autonomy. No longer content to live under constant supervision, many of them yearned for freedom and independence, questioning why they should remain confined to Kantu Labs when they were just as intelligent and capable as the humans around them. The prospect of sentients seeking self-determination was not something Kantu had initially accounted for, and it posed a significant ethical dilemma. What had started as a controlled experiment was now evolving into a social issue, one that would soon challenge the very foundation of human-sentient relations.

While Kantu Labs grappled with the question of sentient

independence, another challenge arose. This time, emerging from a rival research company. Admyre Dynamics, a rapidly growing competitor, made headlines when they successfully uplifted the first fully aquatic sentient: an octopus. They didn't stop there. In the following years, they continued to push the limits, uplifting a variety of new predatory species, including otters, foxes, badgers, and wolves. The emergence of alpha predators as sentients quickly sparked public concern, igniting debates about the ethical boundaries of uplift research and the prospect of regulations. Would these creatures be able to coexist peacefully with humans? Were they inherently more dangerous than the herbivores and omnivores that had come before them?

The arrival of predator sentients diminished the public's initial enthusiasm for uplift research as it gave way to questions about safety, ethics, and the future. The sentients, once viewed as scientific wonders, were now beginning to be seen by some as potential threats, and both Kantu Labs and Admyre Dynamics faced increasing scrutiny from government and advocacy groups.

By the end of the decade, Kantu Labs had expanded its operations dramatically. Six new city-sized facilities were established worldwide, each designed not only to develop new sentients but also to serve as massive, integrated communities where sentients could grow and live alongside their human handlers. The new campuses were built not only to further uplifting research but also to address the mounting concerns about the sentients' place in a human-dominated world. Isolated from human society, the labs functioned as peaceful sanctuaries, dedicated to fostering an artificial harmony between humans and sentients. But the question of whether sentients could ever truly roam free remained unanswered.

The Conflicts (540–556 A)

The early 540s marked a significant turning point in history. While the world came to terms with its first encounters with intelligent extraterrestrial life, and as mankind adapted to the delicate sociopolitical relations that resulted, the balance between humans and sentients began to unravel. What had once been a promising era of scientific advancement and mutual coexistence was rapidly giving way to unrest. The sentients, now adults and numbering in the many thousands, were no longer content to live in the controlled environments of research labs. As more of them matured, their demands for freedom and autonomy grew louder. They wanted to live outside the walls that had both nurtured and essentially imprisoned them. But the public's concern about welcoming predatory sentients into their cities and neighborhoods only intensified. Just a decade later, the same people who once marveled at talking animals now began to fear them as their numbers increased, questioning what they were capable of if left unchecked.

In 542 A, the simmering tension boiled over when a group of sentients successfully staged an escape from the New London lab. While no one was harmed, the breakout sparked widespread panic across the city. The news media sensationalized the event, framing the escapees as a serious threat to the public, despite no evidence of any danger being evident. While authorities scrambled to capture the non-human fugitives, the fear of sentients roaming free in urban areas became a national frenzy. Many began to question the wisdom of uplifting animals in the first place.

In response to the public outcry, the Anetian government took immediate and decisive action, seizing control of all Kantu Labs facilities and forcefully removing Dr. Amari Kantu from his position. Public exhibits of sentients were permanently shut down, and the once transparent policies of Kantu's programs were replaced by strict governmental oversight.

Despite the government's authoritarian response, Kantu's vision was far from extinguished. Expecting such an event to be a possibility, Kantu privately funded the construction of a secret compound deep in the remote countryside of Kazakhstan capable of housing tens of thousands of sentients. In a clandestine operation, he, along with many of his closest associates, smuggled many of the sentients to the hidden facility. It became a safe haven for the uplifted animals who were lucky enough to escape the government seizures. There, Kantu continued his work in the shadows, determined to protect his enormous family of sentients from the growing hostility they were now facing.

With Kantu Labs entirely under government management, the Anetian military saw an opportunity. Recognizing the potential of sentient species, particularly predatory ones, the military began its own secretive uplifting programs with the assistance of Admyre Dynamics. They focused on creating sentient soldiers, selectively uplifting alpha predators for use in combat scenarios. Wolves, large cats, and other predatory species were conscripted into a life of military service, often against their will. Meanwhile, the rest of the sentients not used as disposable tools of war remained sequestered in the labs, subjected to harsh conditions and abuse from their newly appointed handlers. This only ignited resentment among the uplifted population.

As the exploitation of sentients escalated, so too did the frequency of conflicts. Frustrated and embittered, groups of sentients began to rebel, staging small-scale uprisings and escape attempts. Some managed to flee their oppressors, seeking refuge in cities or retreating into the wilderness. There, they hid in the shadows, relying on one another for survival. In the wilderness, small groups grew into secluded communities. In urban areas, many found sanctuary with sympathetic humans willing to offer them shelter, often disguising them as exotic pets. As years passed, the presence of sentients in cities began to increase, and all were disregarded and feared by the masses.

The subjugation of the sentients worldwide finally reached a devastating tipping point in the early 550s. In a desperate move, reacting to relentless acts of abuse, the Morgannen Lab was overtaken violently by the sentients. Its staff and military personnel were held hostage for weeks as the sentients called for their freedom. For a moment, it seemed as though they could finally achieve their goal of liberation. But that hope was short-lived. The military finally responded with overwhelming force, deploying a barrage of autonomous drones to crush the rebellion. What followed was a massacre. Over two thousand sentients were killed in the brutal assault. As the smoke cleared, their bodies were left strewn across the campus grounds as a grim reminder of the consequences of defiance. This uprising, while tragic, marked the beginning of a deep-seated hostility between humans and sentients. Many would regard it as the true beginning of the Sentient War—one that would remain cold for many years to come.

By the beginning of the decade, the global sentient population had swelled to tens of thousands. Many remained under strict military control, while others lived in cities or hid in remote wilderness areas. Public fear and resentment toward sentients continued to grow, fueled by sensationalized media reports of sentient attacks on humans, most of which were retaliatory responses to mistreatment. Calls for harsh action against sentients echoed through the halls of government as society wrestled with how to coexist with beings both like them yet profoundly different.

With his death, the peaceful coexistence once envisioned by Dr. Kantu had crumbled, giving way to an era of suspicion, violence, and division. And as the sentients fought for their right to exist on their own terms, the world braced for the inevitable conflict that would soon engulf them all.

Abolition (556–562 A)

In the year 556 A, the Anetian government responded to the growing unrest with an iron fist. The newly elected Chancellor, Haley Pope, ran on a platform of restoring order and eliminating the "sentient problem" once and for all. True to his word, his administration swiftly enacted sweeping Sentient Abolition Laws, which marked a decisive and brutal turn in the already tense human-sentient relations. The laws went far beyond previous measures. They not only banned all further uplifting, making the process illegal with severe penalties for any violations, but they also mandated the forcible removal of sentients from human homes and public spaces.

Under the draconian laws, sentients who had integrated into human society, some of whom had lived alongside humans for years as family members or trusted companions, were now considered contraband. Police and military personnel were dispatched to round up sentients from cities, suburbs, and even rural areas, dragging them from the homes of those humans who had dared to shelter them. In many cases, sentients were forcibly relocated to remote, inhospitable wilderness regions where survival was uncertain at best. The official narrative claimed it was a form of "compassionate exile," a way for sentients to live freely in the wild. But the reality was, without the experience to survive on their own, and without the help from other sentients, many perished from exposure, starvation, or predatory threats in the isolated regions.

In more extreme cases, overzealous police and military units took matters into their own hands. Some sentients, rather than being relocated, were executed on sight—shot in the streets or in their homes. The executions were often justified by the authorities as necessary to maintain public safety, but the reality was, it was outright murder fueled by the dehumanizing rhetoric. The public, already conditioned by years of anti-sentient propaganda, turned a blind eye to the violence, and in some cases, even cheered it on.

For sentients, the only hope of survival lay in escape. In the midst of the crackdown, a mass exodus of sentients began. Thousands fled in search of refuge, often risking everything for their livelihoods. While some sought their safety in remote wilderness communities, Kazakhstan, which had remained a hidden sanctuary, became the most sought-after destination. But as the exodus grew, so did the surveillance by authorities. Eventually, the Anetian military discovered the facility's location. In a crushing raid, troops stormed the compound, overwhelming its defenses with oppressive force. Both sentients and humans alike were detained or killed, but most others managed to escape, once again displaced from the only place they had known as home to seek shelter far from Aneti's reach.

It was a dark time for early generations of sentients. But as often happens in times of great oppression, an underground movement began to take root. Groups formed, militias rose, and human allies joined in to protect the hidden sentients. Among them, rogue scientists, many of them former employees of Kantu Labs, formed illegal laboratories, and a black market for uplifting emerged. Desperate for their sapiency to live on in future generations, expecting sentient mothers turned to these labs so they would not have to face the prospects of raising non-sentient offspring, otherwise referred to as yamals. The process was risky, but for a sentient, it was a risk worth taking.

At the same time, the streets began to fill with the voices of dissent. Protests erupted across Aneti as humans took to the streets to speak out against the injustice. While some had always viewed sentients as inferior, a growing number recognized the cruelty of separating sentient families and stripping sentients of their rights and lives. Riots broke out in major cities, fueled by the grief and rage of those who had lost loved ones to the abolition laws. Entire neighborhoods became war zones as clashes between protesters and law enforcement escalated into violent confrontations.

In the face of overwhelming adversity, the sentients' future looked bleak. Yet, even in the darkest of times, the flames of resistance remained. The seeds of rebellion had been planted, and though many sentients were too afraid or too weak to fight back, the rest were quietly preparing for what would come next. Though the nation had shown them no mercy, they had not yet lost their will to survive. Hidden in the wilderness and scattered across cities, sentients began to organize, laying the groundwork for a resistance that would soon rise against the oppression seeking to erase them. A war was soon on the horizon.

But the war never came.

The New Era (562 A and Beyond)

In the year 562 A, a newly elected chancellor, Tomas Bakyr, rose to power after Haley Pope's removal from office, bringing with him a glimmer of hope for the sentients who had long suffered under the oppressive Sentient Abolition Laws. The new leader, with the backing of a more progressive Senate, moved swiftly to overturn the policies, marking a pivotal moment in sentient history. The Sentient Laws were enacted, signaling the beginning of a new era of cautious coexistence between humans and sentients. Under these laws, sentients were granted the right to live independently among humans, but their integration into society came with strict regulations designed to control their movements, activities, and interactions. It was a compromise that allowed for sentient autonomy but also reinforced the existing power structures that kept them under human authority.

Among these laws, the 8th Sentient Law marked the end of uplifting exploration as the ring-tailed lemur was the last species to be uplifted.

The Sentient Laws introduced a period of tentative optimism, but they also paved the way for a new form of segregation. Across the world, cities rapidly restructured themselves, designating specific districts for sentient habitation. Some districts became sanctuaries and safe havens where sentients could live, work, and socialize freely. These areas became home to sentient-run schools, businesses, and cultural institutions that allowed uplifted beings to begin forming their own communities. For the first time, sentients had the opportunity to cultivate a sense of independence and progress, to build something more than just survival.

But for every district that welcomed sentients, there were many more that restricted them or shut them out entirely. Discrimination was rife, and while the Sentient Laws granted basic rights, enforcement was often spotty and inconsistent, leaving many uplifted beings vulnerable to harassment, abuse, and exploitation, primarily from the vague interpretations of the second law. Despite these challenges, the seeds of sentient self-determination had been planted and were beginning to take root.

As sentient communities expanded, so did sentient nations, many of which had taken shape during the abolition era while in exile. Across the globe, fledgling sentient-led territories began to emerge: the Corvid Nation in the Caribbean, the feline-led Nikita in western South America, the rat-populated Iratti near India, the kangaroo region of K'jurn in southern Australia, the chimpanzee nation of O'gn'artan bordering the primate state of Elun Aneti in Africa, and Ceta, the oceanic empire of dolphins and octopi. These nations varied greatly in size, influence, and governance. Some were small, peaceful enclaves serving as sanctuaries for specific species, while others were vast territories with full diplomatic recognition. What united them all was a shared vision: to create homelands where sentient species could thrive independently of human control, building futures founded on their own values and aspirations. It was an ambitious dream that many Anetian officials viewed with hesitation, but it could no longer be dismissed as the sentient population surpassed 50 million by the century's end.

As sentients became a more visible and organized force within society, movements advocating for their equal rights began to gain momentum. Sentient rights organizations formed, growing into powerful advocates for legal recognition, equality, and the dismantling of the systemic discrimination sentients still faced. Public opinion was slow to change, but change it did, thanks to the tireless efforts of these organizations, as well as the undeniable contributions sentients made to society in areas such as science, art, and business.

In the decades that followed, society slowly began to shift toward a greater acceptance of sentients. Educational opportunities for uplifted beings emerged as schools and universities began to open their doors to sentient students. Economic participation also grew, with sentient-owned businesses becoming more common and uplifted beings finding employment in various industries. The integration of sentients among humankind gradually reshaped societal attitudes, as newer generations of humans came to recognize sentients not as novelties or predatory threats, but as equal contributors. However, despite the progress made, not all shared these beliefs, and the path toward complete acceptance was far from over.

Challenges persisted, as disparity and prejudice remained deeply rooted in many areas. Sentients still faced barriers to equal treatment under the new laws, and many places continued to enforce segregation. Hate groups and far-right activists continued their calls to return to the days before uplifting. Public discourse was also divided, with some embracing the idea of a shared future with sentients, while others remained reluctant or outright hostile to the notion of non-humans having an equal standing.

As the sentient population increased and their societal presence strengthened, it became apparent that sentients were approaching yet another pivotal moment in history. The struggle for equal rights had gained ground, but the fight was far from over. Beneath the surface of the progress made, there remained a resistance that urged for an end to the Age of Sentients and the reestablishment of human dominance. The question remained: would the world continue to move forward toward unity and equality, or would fear and hatred once again push sentients to the brink of their extinction?

The years ahead would determine the answer.

ABOUT THE AUTHOR

Known also as EmptySet, M.T. Sett is a California-based creator whose work spans art, music, and fiction. Though new to the landscape of published authors, he has pursued literary fiction writing since childhood.

Raised in Southern California, his initial inspiration for writing came from his father, who was both an avid reader and a self-driven writer. He picked up the proverbial pen and began his first novel at the age of twelve. It was far from a masterpiece, but the interest remained. He would later go on to write many more unpublished stories and novels earning him years of practice in the craft.

An ambitious artist, his aspirations include playing guitar, drawing, painting, composing, and producing music. He has also devoted his life studying mathematics, science, programming, and web development while finding comforts and entertainment within the furry fandom. Numerous creative endeavors like these might have scattered another's focus, but not Sett. Instead, his many interests have combined to fuel a science-fiction universe he simply could ignore no longer.

After completing the For All album 'Sentience,' from which this story is derived, Sett returned to literary fiction with renewed purpose. The story you're holding is part of that growing world. The rest, as they say, is history… or perhaps the future!

www.ingramcontent.com/pod-product-compliance
Lightning Source LLC
Chambersburg PA
CBHW060621310726
48982CB00003B/633

* 9 7 8 1 9 7 1 0 8 8 0 1 3 *